KT-431-351

C333904742

To the faculty, staff, and children of Shaaray Tefila Nursery School

First published 2016 by Walker Books Ltd, 87 Vauxhall Walk, London SE11 5HJ • © 2016 Steve Light • The right of Steve Light to be identified as author/illustrator of this work has been asserted by him in accordance with the Copyright, Designs and Patents Act 1988 • This book has been typeset in Stempel Schneidler • Printed in China • 10 9 8 7 6 5 4 3 2 1
All rights reserved. No part of this book may be reproduced, transmitted or stored in an information retrieval system in any form or by any means, graphic, electronic or mechanical, including photocopying, taping and recording, without prior written permission from the publisher. • British Library Cataloguing in Publication Data: a catalogue record for this book is available from the British Library • ISBN 978-1-4063-6776-8 • www.walker.co.uk

FSC
www.fsc.org
MIX
Paper from
responsible sources
FSC™ C020056

SWAP!

STEVE LIGHT

WALKER BOOKS
AND SUBSIDIARIES
LONDON · BOSTON · SYDNEY · AUCKLAND

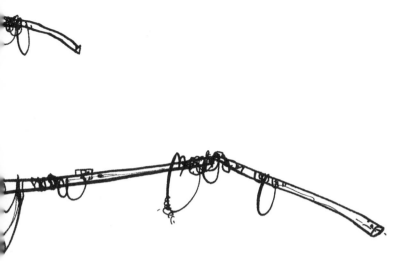

An old ship.

A sad friend.

One button for
two teacups.
SWAP!

Two teacups for
three coils of rope.

SWAP!

Two coils of rope
for six oars.

SWAP!

Two oars for four flags.

SWAP!

One flag for three anchors.

SWAP!

Two anchors for nine sails.

SWAP!

Two sails for
two ship's wheels.

SWAP!

One ship's wheel for three hats.

One hat for three birds.

SWAP!

One bird for
one carved figurehead.

A new ship.

A happy friend.